Pinky Doodle Bug

Elizabeth Hamilton-Guarino

WALDORF PUBLISHING

Published by Waldorf Publishing
2140 Hall Johnson Road
#102-345
Grapevine, Texas 76051
www.WaldorfPublishing.com

Pinky Doodle Bug

ISBN: 978-1-63625-291-9

Library of Congress Control Number: 2020937475

Copyright © 2020

Illustrations by Vova Kirichenko
Design by Baris Celik

For Quinn

Thank you to Kris Fuller who jumped into
Pinky Doodle Bug's world with enthusiasm!
This book wouldn't be possible without you.

Pinky Doodle Bug loved to doodle and draw.
She doodled things in her mind and on things that she saw.

She doodled on this and she doodled on that.
She doodled on everything she could see and everywhere she sat.

As she doodled, she thought there was something amiss; it was a thought she could not dismiss.

So, she called out for help from her friends, the birds, who answered her call with lots of kind words.

The birds of the forest flew in from the trees.
They landed on branches and boulders with ease.

The birds chirped, "You need stories and tales to go with your art."

"I do need your help," said Pinky, "Will you do your part?"

That night as they gathered, she heard them agree,

"Your doodles are amazing,
the world needs to see,

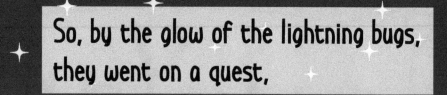

So, by the glow of the lightning bugs, they went on a quest,

to find the best stories ever,
the very best of the best.

Clara the Caterpillar was eager to share.

Sally the Spider piped up with care.

Pete the Porcupine talked about "The Great Trail."

While Fred the Fox
told a tall tale.

Murphy the Moose and Baxter the Bee,
told a cute story about Maine and the sea.

While Betty the Butterfly and Benji the Bunny shared stories with jokes that were really quite funny.

Each story was written as it was told.

Your words are perfect, just for me –

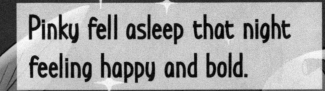

Pinky fell asleep that night feeling happy and bold.

She woke up to voices loud like a band.
Word had spread far across the land.

Pinky fell asleep that night feeling happy and bold.

She woke up to voices loud like a band.
Word had spread far across the land.

I'll doodle each story for all to see.

Her friends watched as Pinky smiled and drew.

When she finished, they all cheered, "Woo-hoo!"

Together they had so much fun.

By combining their talents, they got so much more done.

They followed their hearts
and let their dreams fly.

The End...
But not the end of
Pinky's adventures...

Doodle Pages

Doodle Pages

Doodle Pages

CPSIA information can be obtained
at www.ICGtesting.com
Printed in the USA
LVHW061001251020
669744LV00001B/1